KU-024-897

DRAGLINS
AND THE
FIRE!

VIVIAN FRENCH   CHRIS FISHER

ORCHARD BOOKS

For Abby, with love
x VF

For Glenn and Sam, with love
CF

/ / MAR 2008

CAVAN COUNTY LIBRARY
ACC. No. C/224179
CLASS No. ....J-9-...
INVOICE NO. ...7687..../...
PRICE......6.9.52...

ORCHARD BOOKS
338 Euston Road, London NW1 3BH
Orchard Books Australia
Level 17/207, Kent Street, Sydney, NSW 2000
First published in Great Britain in 2007
First paperback publication 2008
Text © copyright Vivian French 2007
Illustrations © copyright Chris Fisher 2007
The rights of Vivian French and Chris Fisher to be
identified as the author and illustrator of this work
have been asserted by them in accordance with
the Copyright, Designs and Patents Act, 1988.

A CIP catalogue record for this book is
available from the British Library.

ISBN 978 1 84362 701 2 (hardback)
ISBN 978 1 84362 710 4 (paperback)

1 3 5 7 9 10 8 6 4 2 (hardback)
1 3 5 7 9 10 8 6 4 2 (paperback)
Printed in England by Antony Rowe Ltd, Chippenham, Wiltshire
Orchard Books is a division of Hachette Children's Books,
an Hachette Livre UK company.
www.orchardbooks.co.uk

CHAPTER ONE

CAVAN COUNTY LIBRARY

"**M**ine's bigger than yours," Dennis boasted. "Look! It's HUGE!"

Danny watched the smoke ring circling Dennis's head. "Mine was thicker," he said hopefully.

"Rubbish!" Dennis sat back to admire his creation as it slowly floated up into the evening air.

Daffodil snorted. "Bet I can blow a bigger one than either of you." She took a deep breath and shut her eyes as she concentrated. A wisp of smoke escaped from the corner of her mouth, followed by a thick white cloud as Dennis flung himself on her and began to tickle her.

"DAFFODIL!" Dora, arriving to tell her brothers and sister that supper was nearly ready, gazed at the smoke in horror. "You KNOW we're not allowed! That's

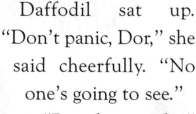

REALLY dangerous!"

Daffodil sat up. "Don't panic, Dor," she said cheerfully. "No one's going to see."

"But they might!" Dora clasped her hands together in agitation. "Aunt Plum always says you never ever know when a Human Beanie might be watching, and they'll come running if they see smoke!" She went pale. "What if they've seen us already?"

"They won't have," Dennis told her. "And they never come down here, anyway – it's too full of prickly stuff." He waved an arm at the trails of ivy and wild blackberry looped round the old and broken-down shed that hid their home. "The uncles really knew what they were doing when they moved into Under Shed."

Dora tried hard not to look doubtful. She

could remember all too clearly when her family had lived in Under Roof, at the top of the tall tenement building that shadowed the far end of the overgrown garden. There had been no cats, no dogs – none of the many fierce and ferocious beasts that regularly gave her horrible nightmares.

It might have been boring, and always the same, but it had felt wonderfully safe – at least, it had until the dreadful day when Uncle Damson had announced that they had to move, because humans were going to develop the flat below their roof space.

Under Shed was beginning to feel more like home, but Dora still didn't feel she could relax. And now her brothers and Daffodil were positively ENCOURAGING awful things to happen.

She took a deep breath. "I'll have to tell Uncle Damson and Aunt Plum," she said. "About the smoking. I'm sorry, but I really will."

"WHAT?" Three pairs of eyes stared at her in total disbelief.

Dora went pink. "I'm not being mean – it's because I HAVE to. Don't you see? What if a Human Beanie found us? I'd never ever EVER forgive myself!"

"Dora Draglin," Daffodil said fiercely, "if you sneak on us, I'll never speak to you again!'

"NOR me!" Dennis agreed.

Danny scratched his ear thoughtfully. He was a fair little draglin, and – unlike Daffodil and Dennis – his conscience sometimes

troubled him. The four of them had already had a number of adventures since their arrival at Under Shed, and Dora had never let them down. Sometimes she had been positively heroic. And – Danny almost groaned out loud – she was right about the smoking. It was, after all, the most important rule in any draglin household. Uncle Plant and Uncle Puddle had a large sign hanging in the hallway saying,

"If you're angry, don't puff –

A wisp of smoke can be enough!"

Danny suddenly saw a clever way out. "Supposing we promised that we'd never smoke again?" he asked.

Dora sighed with relief. She knew Daffodil and Dennis wouldn't carry out their threat of not speaking for ever, but it would be for long enough to make her feel completely miserable.

"OK," she said. "I won't tell."

"Just a minute!" Daffodil folded her arms. "I'M not promising! I want to blow a bigger smoke ring than Dennis!"

"And I'M not promising either," Dennis said flatly. "So there."

CHAPTER TWO

Danny looked at Dora, Dennis and Daffodil as they glared at each other. If he didn't think of something fast there would be terrible consequences. Once Dora had made her mind up she could be just as determined as either Dennis or Daffodil, and she would undoubtedly carry out her threat.

Danny shivered. The idea of Aunt Plum, Uncle Puddle, Uncle Plant and Uncle Damson ALL being furious was not one he fancied. The punishments would be dreadful, and as it was the beginning of the school holidays they would probably be grounded at home for days and DAYS – and he, Dennis and Daffodil had wonderful plans for adventures.

Danny looked round, desperate to find something that would distract the others.

They were sitting on the wooden floor of the old shed, surrounded by broken flowerpots, old leaves, and bits of wood. Underneath was their home; to reach their own front door all the little draglins had to do was scramble off the floor, climb over the end of a drainpipe, and slide down a makeshift ladder before making their way through the uncles' storage space.

It was the pipe that now caught Danny's eye; where did it come from? He looked up, and saw that it disappeared behind the remains of an ivy covered wall. And there was something else up there – but what was it? He screwed up his eyes…

"LOOK! There's a WATER TANK!" Danny leapt to his feet, pointing upwards. Daffodil, Dennis and Dora jumped up too.

"You're RIGHT!" Dennis slapped Danny's back. "Hey! We could go swimming again! Do you remember what fun we used to have in the water tank in Under Roof?"

Daffodil was already heading for the ivy. "Bet you I get there first!"

"I'll bet you you don't!" Dennis was after her at top speed.

Dora felt a huge load lift from her shoulders. For the moment the smoking crisis had been avoided. All the same, now wasn't the moment to go hunting for water tanks. "But we're meant to be going home for supper," she said. "And Aunt Plum's grumpy because she's got an awful cold..."

"Who cares about supper?" Daffodil called as she swung her way up, closely followed by Dennis.

"YOU should," said a deep growly voice, and Uncle Plant appeared beside Dora. He looked reproachfully at her. "Your aunt's worried you've got lost, you've been so long."

Dora blushed. "Sorry," she said.

Uncle Plant grunted, and peered at Daffodil and Dennis. "All your fault, I expect," he remarked. "Trying to look at the cistern, are you? Forgot to tell you that was there. Used to have the odd swim when I was younger, but I'm too fat to climb up now." He laughed. "Had to block the end off, me and Puddle did. Kept dripping onto our stores. Proper nuisance it was. Come and have your supper. It'll still be here tomorrow." And he stomped off.

Daffodil and Dennis whizzed back down, grinning cheerfully. "It's EVER so easy to get there," Dennis reported. "Let's get up really early tomorrow, and have a swim before breakfast!"

"YEAH!" Daffodil punched the air, and Danny and Dora nodded.

CHAPTER THREE

When Dennis said really early he meant it. Even Daffodil was still asleep when Dennis came hurtling into her and Dora's bedroom.

"Go away!" she muttered crossly, and Dora curled herself into an even tighter ball.

"It's still dark..." she mumbled.

"No it's not!" Dennis protested, even though the sun was hardly in the sky. "We're going swimming, remember!"

Daffodil sat up and rubbed her eyes. "OK." She leant over and prodded Dora. "Dor – WAKE UP!"

"The water'll be freezing," Dora said, without moving. "I'll come later."

Daffodil slid off her sleeping mat, and pulled a jumper over her pyjamas. "Where's Danny?"

Dennis made a face. "He said it was the middle of the night."

"We'll have it all to ourselves, then," Daffodil said. "Come on!" And she and Dennis left the snoozing Dora, and crept down the hallway and out of the house.

Outside it was very cold, and very still. Only the earliest birds were cheeping as Dennis and Daffodil hurried past the uncles' stores, climbed the ladder, and reached the old drainpipe.

"Hang on a mo'," Daffodil said as Dennis began to swing himself over it. "I want to see if we can get inside." She crouched down, and crawled into the bottom. A moment later she emerged, shaking her head. "Uncle Plant was right," she reported, "it's blocked up. Wouldn't it be great if we could clear it? We could zoom up to the water tank without having to climb the ivy! Maybe we could have a go after our swim."

Dennis looked at her in amazement.
"Daffy," he said, "didn't you see where the
pipe went?"

"Of course I did!" Daffodil snapped.
"Up to the water tank! That's why—"
She stopped. "OH! You mean, if we

unblocked the pipe, all the water would come flooding out?"

"WOW! Well DONE!" Dennis crossed his eyes. "Careful you don't overstrain your brain!"

Daffodil picked up a handful of moss and threw it at him. "Last one in the water's a sissy!" she challenged, and took off as fast as she could go. Dennis yelled, "Cheat!" and dashed after her.

Dora was right. The water was VERY cold. Daffodil thrashed around wildly, her teeth chattering. If Dennis hadn't been splashing beside her she'd have got straight out; as it was, she felt obliged to stay in until he said he'd had enough.

"Isn't this fun?" Dennis asked, shivering uncontrollably.

Daffodil nodded. She couldn't risk saying anything in case her chattering teeth gave her away.

"Danny and Dora don't know what

they're missing," Dennis said, and pulled himself out.

Hastily following him, Daffodil grabbed at her jumper and wriggled inside. Her wet pyjamas hung clammily round her, but at least the sun was beginning to feel warm on her back.

Dennis began swinging his arms to try and restore some feeling. "We'll have to bring Pip up here," he said. "He'd love it!"

"We could have water p-p-p-parties," Daffodil suggested.

Dennis gave her a superior look. "You're not cold, are you?"

"Of course not," Daffodil said crossly. "I'm warm as toast!"

"Oh yeah?" Dennis settled himself more securely on the rim of the old water cistern. "Bet you can't blow a smoke ring!"

"CAN SO!" Daffodil countered, and puffed up her cheeks. Nothing happened.

Dennis grinned, and blew a perfect smoke ring into the clear morning air, followed quickly by another that soared through the centre of the first.

Daffodil couldn't help being impressed. "WOW!" she said. "Will you show me how to do that?"

Dennis's answer was lost in the roar from down below.

"DENNIS! Down here THIS MINUTE!"

CHAPTER FOUR

Dennis was in disgrace. So was Daffodil. She had told Uncle Damson that she would have been blowing smoke rings as well if she hadn't been so cold and wet. Danny tried to confess that he'd been joining in the day before, but Uncle Damson turned a furious shade of purple and refused to believe him.

"You four always stick together," he said angrily. "Dora will be telling me she was blowing fire in a minute! No, I know what I saw. Dennis and Daffodil are grounded for a week, and I'm sending the mowser and Daffodil's beetle away."

Dennis and Daffodil were shocked into paying attention. They stared at Uncle Damson in horror.

"But you can't!" Daffodil gasped. "He'll pine for me!"

"And Hero isn't just mine – she's Danny's too!" Dennis protested.

"You should have thought about that before you put all our lives in danger," Uncle Damson snapped.

Uncle Puddle shook his head solemnly. "Bad behaviour has a nasty habit of making others suffer."

"That's right," Uncle Plant growled. "We thought we could trust you to go Outdoors, and now it seems we can't."

For almost the first time in their entire

lives Dennis and Daffodil felt genuinely sorry for what they'd done. They hung their heads, and muttered, "We won't do it again. Promise."

Aunt Plum saw the tears rolling down Daffodil's nose. "If you can prove you've learnt your lesson," she said, "we'll see about letting you have your pets back." She stopped, and sneezed loudly. "ATCHOO! Excuse me. Now, you're to stay in your rooms, and there'll be NO nonsense. Understood?"

"Yes, Aunt Plum." Daffodil and Dennis trailed dismally away.

Aunt Plum blew her nose, and turned to Danny and Dora. "Why don't you two take little Pip for a swim?" she suggested.

"Thank you, Aunt Plum," Dora said, but without enthusiasm.

Pip, quite unaware of the heavy black cloud hanging over his cousins, heard the word swim. "Rah!" he  shouted. "Rah! Swim swim SWIM!" And he grabbed Danny and Dora's hands and began dragging them towards the door.

Aunt Plum watched him fondly as she blew her nose yet again. "I'll make you a picnic lunch," she said. "You can pop back and collect it later. Now, DO make sure you keep your eyes and ears open, and

DON'T go any further than the tank."

"Any more trouble, and you'll all be grounded for good," Uncle Damson threatened. "I never have approved of you running around outside Under Shed! School and home, home and school – that's all silly young draglins should be allowed!"

"I'm sure they'll be very careful," Aunt Plum said soothingly. "ATCHOOO!! And they aren't going far."

Uncle Damson harrumphed, and strode away. "I'm going Collecting with Plant and Puddle!" he called over his shoulder. "Puddle says the nuts are ripe. We'll be back this afternoon."

CHAPTER FIVE

O nce they were out in the sunshine Dora began to feel better, but Danny was weighed down with guilt.

"It's not YOUR fault Uncle Damson didn't believe you," Dora told him.

"I should be indoors with Dennis," Danny sighed.

Dora had a flash of intuition. "Maybe Uncle Damson didn't WANT to believe you," she said. "He knew that if you were together you wouldn't mind being grounded!"

"H'm." Danny looked thoughtful. "You might be right. You are clever, Dor."

Dora smiled with pleasure, but said, "Not really. Let's have this swim. I'm boiling!"

"SWIM!" yelled Pip, and they headed up the ivy.

They were nearly at the top when Dora

suddenly stopped. "What's that noise?"

Danny paused to listen. "I can't hear anything."

"It was a rustling noise," Dora whispered anxiously. "Oh, Danny! Do you think it could be a chat?"

"Honestly, Dor, I can't hear anything." Danny gave Pip a final heave up to the edge of the water tank. "At least, nothing odd. Maybe it was a brid—"

"It didn't sound like a brid. It was more

like a huge aminal stamping about." Dora hung off the ivy, and scanned the world below. "I can't see anything – OH!" She let out a squeal. "DANNY! There's a BEANIE – it's coming this way! Oh NO! There's another one as well!"

Danny was distracted by Pip, who had pulled his clothes off and was demanding to go in the water. As soon as he was happily splashing Danny peered down, and saw Dora was right. Two boys were fighting their

way through the brambles and long grass.

"What shall we DO?" Dora squeaked in Danny's ear.

"Stay still," Danny hissed back. "They'll never see us behind the ivy!"

Dora gave a muffled wail. "What if they saw Dennis's smoke? What if they're coming to look for us?"

"Actually," Danny said slowly, "I think they're looking for somewhere to hide…"

Danny was right. Once the boys had reached a small clearing in amongst the bushes they crouched down, and began to empty their pockets. The two little draglins stared in wonder.

"What are they doing?" Dora whispered.

Danny didn't answer. His eyes grew wide as he saw one of the boys scratch at a small box, and a bright flame leapt upwards. The other boy leant forwards, and lit a white tube that he held to his mouth. As the first faint trails floated upwards,

Danny grabbed Dora's arm.

"DOR!" he gasped in horror. " I know what they're doing! They're SMOKING!"

"Don't be silly…" Dora began, but Danny was right. The boys were puffing clouds of smoke into the air, and grinning cheerfully at each other.

"What if they set fire to the bushes?"

Dora clutched urgently at Danny's arm. "What'll we DO?"

Danny shrugged. "Don't know."

Dora gritted her teeth. "We've got to stop them! There must be SOMETHING we can think of..."

"Cool hide-out," one of the boys said, his voice very clear.

"Yeah." The second boy lay back. "My dad'll never find us in among this lot."

"Nor mine." The other laughed, then coughed. "He'd kill me if he knew what I was up to."

A movement in the distance caught Danny's eye, and he let out a long low whistle.

"Dora," he said, "have a look at this!"

CHAPTER SIX

Dora squinted towards the end of the garden.

"Two more Beanies!" she said, and began to tremble. "And they're BIG ones!"

Danny was looking surprisingly calm for a small draglin faced with danger. "Do you know what, Dor?" he asked. "I reckon they're looking for the other ones!" He moved an ivy leaf so he could see better. "They look REALLY angry – the bigger one looks just like Uncle Damson!"

Dora frowned. "He does, doesn't he? So maybe we'd better help him!" And as Danny stared at her incredulously, she put her fingers in her mouth and whistled an ear piercing whistle.

The two men at the far end of the tangled garden snapped upright. They looked towards Dora…

…and they saw the smoke.

"They're in the brambles," yelled the one that looked like Uncle Damson. "Paul! Darren! Come out of there this minute! We know you're there – and we know you're smoking!"

The two boys froze.

"Come out, or we'll come and pull you

out by your hair!"

"It's my dad!" The taller boy was as white as a sheet. He stood up, and hastily flung his half smoked cigarette away, followed by the packet. "C'mon, Paul – we'd better go."

Paul was coughing badly, and holding his head. "OK. Don't feel too good…"

"You'll feel even worse if your dad has to drag you out of here," Darren told him.

Paul struggled to his feet. Danny, completely fascinated, saw his face.

"Did you know Beanies can go green?" he whispered. "Aunt Plum never said."

"He's going to be sick," Dora prophesied, and she was right. When at last Paul was able to stagger after Darren, the two of them made their way to where the men were waiting. There was a great deal of noisy shouting before all four disappeared, and Danny began to laugh.

"Did you hear that?" he chortled. "They've been grounded! It's just like us!"

Dora wasn't sure if she should disapprove

or not. "You and Dennis weren't sick," she said as she helped Pip out of the water tank, and rubbed him dry.

"No." Danny shook his head. "They didn't do the smoke themselves, though, did they? It was those white stick things they put in their mouths."

"Sirrygets," Dora said smugly. "Aunt Plum told us about them in a lesson."

"Mum Plum!" Pip interrupted, and he began scrambling down the ivy. "See Mum Plum!"

Dora started to follow him. "Come on, Danny – let's go. Pip's had enough."

"OK," Danny said, then hesitated. "I might just have a quick swim while I'm here. It's SO hot!"

Halfway down, Dora's nose began to twitch. "Can you smell something burning?" she asked Pip.

"Biscuit!" Pip said.

"I don't think it's Aunt Plum's cooking." Dora sniffed again. "It smells different. Maybe it's left over from the sirrygets…"

"Yeah!" Pip said helpfully. "Biscuit!'

In the far corner of the old wooden shed the cigarette went on smouldering…

CHAPTER SEVEN

Danny and Daffodil were whispering through a small hole in the wall that divided their rooms.

"I'm going MAD," Daffodil hissed. "I'm going to chew up Dora's sleeping mat, I'm so BORED!"

"Me too," Dennis said.

"There must be SOMETHING we can do," Daffodil went on. "Do you think we could escape if we dug a hole in the floor?" Her voice brightened. "HEY! Maybe we could make a tunnel that led into the Underground? We could sneak out and have all kinds of adventures! That would be SO cool! What do you think?"

There was silence from the other side of the wall.

"Dennis?" Daffodil pressed closer to the hole. "DENNIS? Are you LISTENING?"

"ATCHOOO! Dennis is reading a book."
Aunt Plum's voice was sharp. "And I'd
suggest you find something to do as well,
Daffodil."

Daffodil slumped onto the floor. There
was no arguing with Aunt Plum when she
sounded like that. She picked up one of
Dora's precious knitting pins,
and began to scratch
at the floor. After
a moment it was
obvious that any
escape route was
impossible, so she
wandered over to
the window, opened
it, and leant out.
There wasn't much
to see as the window
overlooked the uncles' storage area, but at
least it made a change. Daffodil sighed
heavily, and began picking at the windowsill
with the pin.

A noise made her look up, and she saw Pip and Dora making their way home in between the heaps of nuts and dried berries.

"P'sssst!" she called. "Dora! Over here!"

Dora was looking distracted, and didn't hear. It was Pip who shouted, "'Lo, Daffy!"

Dora jumped, and hurried across to the window. "PLEASE talk to me," Daffodil pleaded. "I'm going MAD! What have you been doing? Have you been swimming?"

Dora shook her head. "No," she said.

"There were these Beanies, and they were smoking sirrygets, but they went away." She pulled a snow-white hankie out of her pocket, and blew her nose. "It's really odd. I can't stop smelling it – the smoke, I mean."

Daffodil hauled herself as far out of the window as she could without actually falling, and sniffed.

"Naah," she said. "You're imagining – " she paused, and sniffed again. "Actually, I CAN smell something!"

With a wriggle and a squeeze she was out of the window. "Quick!" she said, "we've got to get Dennis out here too!" And she furtively peered into the next window along. There was no sign of Aunt Plum, and Dennis was sitting doing nothing. When Daffodil tapped on the window he zoomed over to see what she wanted.

"Dennis, you've got to get out NOW!" Daffodil ordered. "We can smell burning – come ON!"

Dennis needed no second invitation, and in a fraction of a second a stunned Dora found herself being rushed back the way she'd just come.

"What about Pip?" she gasped.

"Just hang on to him," Daffodil ordered. "He's safer here with us – OH! OH! Look at THAT!"

CHAPTER EIGHT

There was no need to tell anyone to look. As the little draglins reached the floor of the shed coils of thick white smoke came creeping across the broken boards towards them, making them cough. Dora screamed, and grabbed Pip.

"The whole shed's on fire!" she shrieked.

"Not yet, it isn't." Danny, soaking wet and covered in smuts, dropped down beside her. "We've GOT to put it out before it really takes hold. I've been sloshing water down from the water tank but I can't get it to go far enough...we need to soak the whole floor!"

"I bet I can!" Daffodil darted for the ivy, but Danny caught her by her tail and pulled her back.

"Hang ON, Daff," he said. "We've got to think—"

"We could bring up water from the house," Dennis suggested, but Danny shook his head. "We couldn't bring enough – not in time—"

"THE PIPE!" Daffodil clutched Dennis's arm. "QUICK! If we can unblock the bottom, all the water'll come out and we can swoosh it EVERYWHERE!" And she flew towards the drainpipe, and scrambled

underneath. Dora's pin was still in her hand, and she began frantically hacking at the solid lump of clay the uncles had used as a seal.

Dennis and Dora rushed after her to help, dragging Pip between them, but Danny stood still. He was staring at what he could see of the pipe, even though behind him small flames were beginning to flicker amongst the smoke.

"Beanies must have put that pipe in," he thought, "but WHY? The water just flows straight from the tank to the ground, and if the uncles hadn't sealed off the end there'd be nothing to stop it…so what was the POINT?" He moved closer, and instead of climbing the ivy, pushed it to one side – and gasped.

There, right above him, was an old tap. It was rusty, and covered in cobwebs and bits of ivy, and nearly as big as Danny – but it was, undoubtedly, a tap.

"DENNIS!" Danny yelled, "DAFFODIL! DORA! COME HERE!"

Dora appeared, a wailing Pip beside her. "They can't come," she puffed, "Daffy says she's nearly got the clay loose!"

"But there's a TAP!" Danny pointed. "If we can turn that—"

From the bottom of the drainpipe came a yell of triumph – and then a dreadful silence.

Dennis crawled out. "There's no water," he said.

"HERE! UP HERE!" Danny was already beside the tap, pushing his hardest. "PLEASE, Dennis! HELP ME! Get Daffy out of there NOW!"

Dennis, Danny and Daffodil heaved and heaved, while Dora held Pip's hand and willed the tap to turn. Behind her the flames began to crackle ominously…

Dora couldn't bear it any longer. "Stay there and don't MOVE!" she told Pip, and she scrambled up to join the others. Grasping the tap handle with Daffodil, while Danny and Dennis pulled on the other side, she took a deep breath. "One two three – NOW!" she shouted...

...and a gushing fountain of water swooshed out of the tap, and rushed across

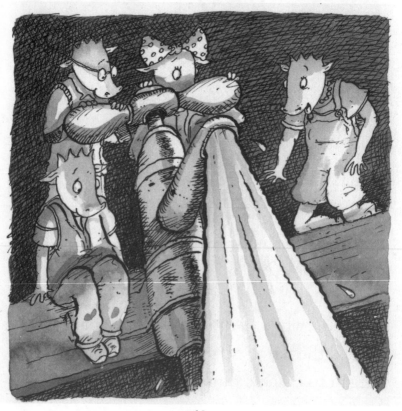

the floorboards. It swept leaves, sticks, and bits of old flowerpot with it, and hit the oncoming flames with a deeply satisfying HISSSSSSSSSS. Dennis, Daffodil and Danny cheered loudly, but Dora's heart was hammering so hard in her chest she could hardly breathe.

"Where's Pip gone?" she whispered urgently. "WHERE'S PIP?"

CHAPTER NINE

The first thing Aunt Plum knew about the danger above was when a drip plopped onto her head from the kitchen ceiling. The drip was followed by another, and then another. Aunt Plum grabbed a bucket, but as she pushed it into place another leak sprang behind her.

"Atchooo! ATCHOOOO! Whatever's going on?" she said, and went to the window, which looked out towards the Underground. There was no sign of rain.

Aunt Plum ran to the door, and hurried outside. At once, even with her cold, she could smell burning – burning mixed with an even stronger smell of charred wet wood. She flew round to the storage space behind the house, and stopped dead in her tracks. Water was pouring from the boards above... but as she stared it began to lessen.

"THE CHILDREN!" Aunt Plum shrieked in terror. "Danny and Dora and Pip! Oh, where ARE they?" And she flung herself up the ladder, dreading what she might see.

What she found made her rub her eyes, and then rub them again. The entire floor of the old shed was soaking wet, and in the far corner was a charred heap of blackened leaves and wood, still hissing faintly. Four little draglins, soaking wet and covered in sooty smuts, were crouching down beside a completely unrecognisable Pip. He was black from top to toe, and yelling, "MINE! MINE!" at the top of his voice.

Aunt Plum swayed, and put her hand on the water pipe to steady herself.

Pip saw her, and his voice grew even shriller.

"MUM PLUM!" He rushed towards her, clutching the last half inch of cigarette. "'S MINE!" he declared, and flung himself into her arms.

Dennis, Daffodil, Dora and Danny stood up, and there was a long silence.

At last Dora said, "Erm...there's been a bit of a fire, Aunt Plum."

"'S all right, though," Dennis grinned. "We put it out."

Aunt Plum, still completely speechless, looked from Pip and the cigarette to the draglins, and then back again.

"It was a Beanie," Daffodil explained. "He was smoking sirrygets – that's what Pip's holding, but he won't give it back."

"We were going to throw it away," Dennis said virtuously. "Smoking is VERY DANGEROUS INDEED."

"Quite right!" Uncle Plant's booming voice came floating up from below, shortly followed by him stumping up the ladder. He was closely followed by Uncle Puddle and

Uncle Damson, laden with two bags of ripe hazelnuts. "Glad you've…" His voice faded away as he looked round him. "Oh, my scaly wailey tail! WHATEVER'S happened?"

"Something to do with these BAD little draglins, without a doubt!" Uncle Damson thundered. "WHAT are Daffodil and Dennis doing here?"

Aunt Plum laid a hand on his arm. "Damson, dear," she said, "I'm not sure of the details, but one thing is VERY clear. These four little draglins have saved Under Shed from burning to the ground. Look – Pip's found the sirryget that started the blaze!"

"MINE!" Pip squealed, and held up his precious prize.

Uncle Damson's eyes bulged as he took in the situation. Uncle Plant and Uncle Puddle marched over to the steaming heap of cinders, and kicked it apart.

"Humph!" Uncle Puddle said gruffly. "Well done! Well done indeed! Always worried something like this might happen, but never guessed it'd be my nephews and nieces that saved the day!"

"AND saved Under Shed!" Uncle Plant agreed.

Dora looked anxiously at Uncle Puddle. "We took the block out from the bottom of the drain," she said. "We didn't know it wouldn't work."

"But then Danny found the tap," Daffodil said.

"But it took all of us to make it turn," Danny added.

Uncle Plant looked at Uncle Puddle. "Did you know there was a tap there, Puddle?"

"Never did, Plant," said Uncle Puddle. "Well done, Danny."

Danny stared at the ground in embarrassment.

"Well well well." Uncle Damson had found his voice again. "Ahem. Yes. Well done." He looked at his grubby nieces and nephews, and the sooty Pip. "I'd say it was time for a nice hot bath, wouldn't you, Plum? And then – ahem – we can see about getting that mowser and the beetle back."

"YES!" shouted Dennis and Daffodil as they punched the air. "THANK YOU, Uncle Damson!"

"RAH!" shouted Pip.

Aunt Plum nodded, and began to smile as she wiped her nose.

"What is it?" Uncle Damson asked, puzzled.

"It's the first time ever that Daffodil and Dennis have been told to have a bath, and they haven't complained," she explained.

"Actually," Dennis said, "actually, I was going to say that we DID have a cleaning sort of swim this morning…"

And even Uncle Damson had to laugh.

CAVAN COUNTY LIBRARY

HAVE YOU READ ALL THE DRAGLINS BOOKS?

Daffodil, Dora, Dennis and Danny
can't believe they are moving to the great
Outdoors! How will they get down from
Under Roof? And will they get to see the
scary chats and dawgs they've
heard so much about?

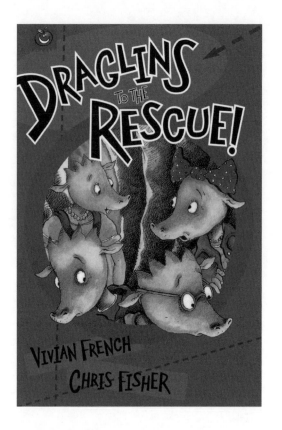

Daffodil, Dora, Dennis and Danny
have moved Outdoors, but their things are
trapped Under Roof! Dennis has a PLAN
to rescue them... But will the gigantic
Human Beanies get in the way?

Wowling has been heard near the draglins'
home in Under Shed! Daffodil, Dora, Dennis
and Danny come face to face with a scary chat
for the first time ever – are four little
draglins a match for terrible
teeth and sharp claws?

What will draglin school in the great
Outdoors be like? Daffodil, Dora, Dennis
and Danny don't know what to expect,
but their classmate Peg does.
She wants to be boss!

Here comes a fierce crow with a big
beak – is this the end of Dennis? It was meant
to be a splendid day out from school, but
he's got himself lost in a field. Will Daffodil,
Dora and Danny find him in time?

Daffodil, Dora, Dennis and Danny are
off to visit Great Grandmother Attica, but
it's a scary journey. Can they save themselves,
let alone a little ducklet lost on the
edge of the Great Wetness?

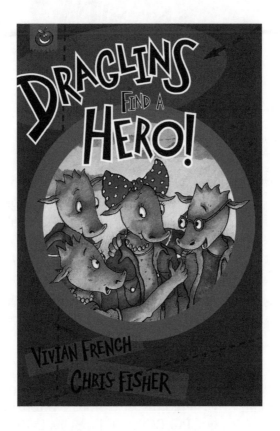

Summer holidays should be fun, but it
hasn't rained in weeks. There are cracks in the
Underground, and Daffodil, Dora, Dennis
and Danny's world is in terrible
danger – what can they do?

by Vivian French
illustrated by Chris Fisher

All priced at £8.99.

Draglins books are available from all good bookshops,
or can be ordered direct from the publisher:
Orchard Books, PO BOX 29, Douglas IM99 1BQ.
Credit card orders please telephone 01624 836000
or fax 01624 837033 or visit our website:
www.orchardbooks.co.uk
or e-mail: bookshop@enterprise.net for details.

To order please quote title, author and ISBN
and your full name and address.
Cheques and postal orders should be made
payable to 'Bookpost plc.'

Postage and packing is FREE within the UK
(overseas customers should add £2.00 per book).

Prices and availability are subject to change.